Community Helpers

Bank Tellers

by Katie Bagley

Consultants:
Shannon Duffy
Executive Director
Minnesota South Central American Institute of Banking

Lois J. Schuldt
Teller
State Bank of Belle Plaine, Minnesota

Bridgestone Books
an imprint of Capstone Press
Mankato, Minnesota

Bridgestone Books are published by Capstone Press
151 Good Counsel Drive, P.O. Box 669, Mankato, Minnesota 56002
http://www.capstone-press.com

1-02-03

Library of Congress Cataloging-in-Publication Data
Bagley, Katie.
     Bank tellers/by Katie Bagley.
        p. cm.—(Community helpers)
     Includes bibliographical references and index.
     ISBN 0-7368-0805-1
        1. Bank tellers—Juvenile literature. [1. Bank tellers. 2. Occupations.] I. Title.
II. Community helpers (Mankato, Minn.)
HG1615.7.T4 B33 2001
332.1'2—dc21

                                                                                    00-009767

Summary: A simple introduction to the work bank tellers do, tools they use, skills they
     need, and their importance to the communities they serve.

Editorial Credits
Sarah Lynn Schuette, editor; Karen Risch, product planning editor; Heather Kindseth,
     cover designer; Heidi Schoof, photo researcher

Photo Credits
Charles Gupton/Pictor, 6; Bob Daemmrich/Pictor, 18
James L. Shaffer, 4, 8, 10, 14, 16, 20
Steve Smith/FPG International LLC, cover; Art Montes De Oca/FPG International LLC, 12

1 2 3 4 5 6 06 05 04 03 02 01

Table of Contents

Bank Tellers 5

What Bank Tellers Do 7

Where Bank Tellers Work 9

Tools Bank Tellers Use 11

Skills Bank Tellers Need 13

Different Kinds of Bank Tellers 15

Bank Tellers and School 17

People Who Help Bank Tellers. 19

How Bank Tellers Help Others 21

Hands On: Money Memory 22

Words to Know 23

Read More 24

Internet Sites 24

Index. 24

Bank Tellers

Bank tellers help customers in banks. They help keep track of balances in bank accounts. A balance is the total amount of money a customer has in an account. Bank tellers also cash checks, make change, and count money.

bank account
a record of the money people put in or take out of a bank

What Bank Tellers Do

Bank tellers are friendly and polite to customers. They help customers put deposits of money into bank accounts. Bank tellers also help customers make withdrawals. They sometimes give customers receipts that show the amount of a deposit.

withdrawal
an amount of money taken out of a bank account

Where Bank Tellers Work

Bank tellers often work at the front counter of a bank. Many banks have their own buildings. These banks sometimes have drive-up windows where bank tellers work. Other banks are in grocery stores, department stores, or shopping malls.

Tools Bank Tellers Use

Bank tellers use computers and calculators to add deposits and to subtract withdrawals. Tellers keep track of money in their cash drawer. Bank tellers also use teller machines to print deposit receipts.

cash drawer

the drawer under a teller's counter that holds bills and coins

Skills Bank Tellers Need

Bank tellers need to have good math and counting skills. They need to handle money carefully. Tellers often put money into a safe or a vault. Bank tellers also need to keep banking records private.

vault

a locked room used to keep money safe

Different Kinds of Bank Tellers

Head tellers make sure all cash drawers have the correct amount of money. The head teller counts this money before the bank opens and after the bank closes. Vault tellers count the money in the vault. Vault tellers often order new currency.

currency
money; vault tellers order new coins and paper bills.

Bank Tellers and School

Many bank tellers learn about bank services and bank rules at work. Students who want to be bank tellers often take math classes in high school. Some bank tellers go to college to learn more about banking.

college
a place where students study after high school

17

People Who Help Bank Tellers

Many people work together in a bank. Head tellers train new tellers. Personal bankers help customers open bank accounts. Bank guards help bank tellers keep people's money safe.

How Bank Tellers Help Others

Bank tellers help people keep track of their money. They help customers fill out bank forms. Bank tellers help to make the bank a comfortable place for customers.

Hands On: Money Memory

Bank tellers count money carefully. This game will help you practice your addition and counting skills.

What You Need

24 index cards
Markers
Four friends
A table

How to Play

1. Shuffle the dollar cards and spread them out face down on a table.

Making Dollar Cards

1. Draw a $1 bill on six index cards.
2. Draw two $1 bills on six index cards.
3. Draw three $1 bills on six more of the index cards.
4. Draw four $1 bills on the last six index cards.

2. A player turns two cards over. If the cards add up to $5, the player keeps the cards in a pile. This pile is the player's "vault." The player takes another turn. If the cards do not total $5, the player turns the cards face down.
3. The game continues until all cards are off the table. The player with the most money in his or her vault at the end of the game wins.

Words to Know

balance (BAL-uhnss)—a total or exact amount of money in a bank account

calculator (KAL-kyuh-lay-tur)—a machine used to figure out math problems

customer (KUHSS-tuh-mur)—a person who visits a store or a business; customers often buy goods or services.

deposit (di-POZ-it)—an amount of money put into a bank account

receipt (ri-SEET)—a piece of paper given to a customer that shows the amount of something

withdrawal (with-DRAW-uhl)—an amount of money taken out of a bank account

Read More

Hall, Margaret. *Banks.* Earning, Saving, Spending. Chicago: Heinemann Library, 2000.

Sirimarco, Elizabeth. *At The Bank.* Field Trips. Chanhassen, Minn.: Child's World, 2000.

Internet Sites

Coin Clubhouse
http://www.usmint.gov/kids/clubhouse/index.html
FDIC Learning Bank
http://www.fdic.gov/about/learn/learning/index.html
Kids Bank
http://www.kidsbank.com
MoneyCents: Making Money Make Sense for Kids
http://www.kidsmoneycents.com

Index

balance, 5
bank accounts, 5, 7, 19
calculators, 11
cash drawer, 11, 15
change, 5
checks, 5
computers, 11

currency, 15
customers, 5, 7, 19, 21
deposit, 7, 11
receipts, 7, 11
teller machines, 11
vault, 13, 15
withdrawals, 7, 11